The Biggest Snowman Ever

by Steven Kroll

Illustrated by Jeni Bassett

SCHOLASTIC INC.

Cartwheel
B·O·O·K·S®

New York   Toronto   London   Auckland   Sydney
Mexico City   New Delhi   Hong Kong   Buenos Aires

For Kathleen
—S.K.

Dedicated to Rachel
—J.B.

Text copyright © 2005 by Steven Kroll.
Illustrations copyright © 2005 by Jeni Bassett Leemis.
All rights reserved. Published by Scholastic Inc.
SCHOLASTIC, CARTWHEEL BOOKS, and associated logos
are trademarks and/or registered trademarks of Scholastic Inc.

ISBN 0-439-66639-2

40 39 38 37

15

Printed in the U.S.A. 40 • First printing, January 2005

Once there were two mice who fell in love with the same snowman, and this is how it happened.

On a bright winter day, the mayor of
Mouseville announced the town snowman contest.
"Whoever makes the biggest snowman will
win a prize!" he declared. All the mice were excited.
"The judging of the contest will take place
in two weeks," said the mayor. "Good luck to
all of you."

"I'm going to make a really big snow princess," said Penelope.
"I'm going to make a really big snow Martian!" said James.

"I'm going to make the biggest snowman ever," said Clayton, the house mouse.

His friend Desmond, the field mouse, frowned. "No, you're not. I'm going to make the biggest snowman ever."

"Oh, yeah?" said Clayton.

"Oh, yeah," said Desmond.

That night, it snowed and snowed. Huge drifts
covered driveways, roads, and fields.

It was the perfect beginning for a snowman contest.

In town, Penelope began her snow princess and James began his snow Martian.

Out in the country, Clayton and Desmond began their snowmen.

Clayton made a snowball and rolled it along the ground. The more he rolled it, the bigger it got. Before long, he had a large base for his snowman.

Not far away, Desmond was doing the same thing.

The next day, Clayton made a huge snowball
for his snowman's belly.

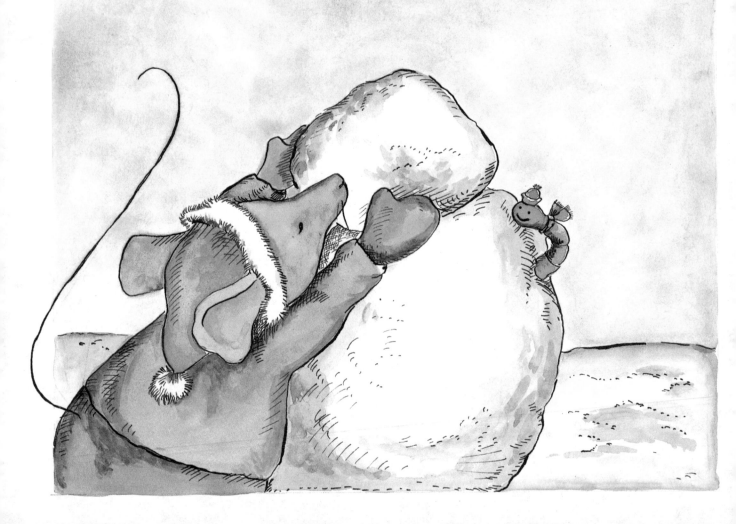

Not far away, Desmond did the same.

That night, Clayton brought his dad out to see his snowman.

Dad scratched his head. "I don't know, son. It's going to be big, but I'm not sure it will be the biggest."

Clayton smiled up at him. "I'm just getting started," he said.

Dad whispered in his ear,
"If you want to work faster, use
a wheelbarrow to carry the snow."

A little later, Desmond brought out his uncle Vernon.

"I don't know," said Vernon. "It's going to be big, but will it be the biggest?"

Desmond smiled. "I'm just getting started," he said.

Vernon whispered in his ear,
"If you want to work faster, use
a wheelbarrow to carry the snow."

The next day, Clayton filled his wheelbarrow with
snow. He piled the snow onto the snowman. Then he
rolled another snowball for the snowman's head.

Not far away, Desmond did the same.

A few days later, Desmond ran into town to look at
James's snow Martian and Penelope's snow princess.
"Hmm," he said, "all of our snowpeople are the
same size."

That afternoon, Clayton made the same discovery.

The next day, while working on his snowman, Clayton had an idea. He brushed the snow off his gloves and walked toward Desmond.

At the same moment, Desmond had an idea. He brushed the snow off his gloves and walked toward Clayton.

They bumped into each other and fell down.

"I have an idea," said Clayton.
"I have an idea," said Desmond.
"We should do this together," said Clayton.
"No one said we couldn't," said Desmond.

First they rolled each part of Desmond's snowman over to the middle of the field.

Then they rolled each part of Clayton's snowman over.

They piled the snowballs on top of one another.
Clayton dropped a floppy hat on the snowman's head.
Desmond added a long scarf, huge coal eyes, and a giant carrot nose.

When they were done, they had
built the biggest snowman ever.

The morning of the contest,
field mice on snowmobiles brought
the judges to the country.

"You both win the prize," said the mayor, handing Clayton and Desmond a large wedge of Swiss cheese. "Let the celebration begin!"

Everyone gathered to dance around the snowman, drink hot chocolate, and eat doughnuts.

"We did it," said Clayton and Desmond,
jumping up and down. "We did it together!"